The Freedom Bridge

John Alexander Reese

The Freedom Bridge

PENDIUM
PUBLISHING HOUSE
514-201 DANIELS STREET
RALEIGH, NC 27605

For information, please visit our Web site at
www.pendiumpublishing.com

PENDIUM Publishing and its logo
are registered trademarks.

THE FREEDOM BRIDGE
by John Alexander Reese

ISBN: 978-1-944348-70-0

PUBLISHER'S NOTE

This book is printed on acid-free paper.

Contents

Acknowledgment

J would first like to give thanks to God for the wonderful opportunity to create this story. Every good and perfect gift comes from the Lord. Secondly, I want to thank my lovely wife (Jan) for her love and support for forty-four years. What an amazing life. You have been my best friend, companion, and the love of my life. Thank you, Sweetie. Thirdly, I'd like to dedicate this book to my children, Antonio and Janelle. It has been a great honor to be your father, Antonio. To my late daughter Janelle, you can't come to me, but one day I will come to you.

Preface

*J*oin these three African American time travelers, Rob, Claire, and Benjamin (Benji), along with their border collie Lucy, on an exciting adventure through our country's past.

While Mom (Audrey James) struggles to keep the kids occupied during the summer vacation, the children immerse themselves in passive entertainment and sheer boredom.

Tag along as a visit to the newly constructed library transforms a boring summer for Rob, Claire, and Benji James into a summer of action, drama, war, and history when an old brass key to a dusty cellar unlocks a portal to the Confederate States in 1864.

Experience the thrill as the James children discover the value of friendship, teamwork, bravery, and their love for each other when they witness history up close and personal.

Chapter 1

It's Your Story, Gloria

*I*t was the evening of July 4th, 1864, somewhere between North Carolina and Virginia. The brilliance and explosion of fireworks could be seen and heard throughout the plantation. Beyond the 4th of July festivity was an unusual stir on the Jamison plantation. Rumors had been swirling all day among the slave quarters that Anna Jamison was back. Why did she come back? Why would she risk her newly found freedom to return to this miserable and hopeless place?

Anna was a runaway slave that had escape to Willingham, Pennsylvania, and won her freedom. What would happen to Anna if Beau Jamison found out his prized cotton picker had returned? Beau Jamison was angry for months after Anna ran away. How in the world did she outsmart Beau? To make matters worse, how had she escaped the clutches of the Railroad men? These men are hired professional slave catchers.

The Jamison family was notable in the cotton and tobacco industries, owning as many as seventy-five slaves. The Jamisons had participated in the slave trade business for decades.

Gloria, Anna's mother, had been on the Jamison plantation since she was a little girl of about six years old. She had been bought by Major Thaddeus Jamison, Beau's father. Gloria had not seen her mother and father since the dreadful day she was separated from them at the auction. Her father, Charles, and mother, Anna Joy, were sold down the river to Mississippi. All she remembered were the cries and tears as the wagon drove away with her. Gloria was given to a slave woman named Mattie, who had a daughter, Beulah, to be raised on the plantation. Major Jamison was not at home much; he was usually away on business. The overseers and Major Jamison's wife, Lydia, managed the plantation until Beau was old enough to take over the business.

When Gloria came to the Jamison plantation, Beau and she were about the same age. The two played together, fought with one another, laughed and cried with each other; they were best friends. Everybody knew the kids liked each other; however, the line between the servant girl and the master's son should never be crossed. Never crossed, but often blurred.

As the two grew older, Beau and Gloria were constantly reminded of what was right and proper. Beau, by his mother, his friends, and the local Southern society. Gloria, by Beau's mother, Mattie, and the other slaves on the plantation who instructed her on what was proper. A public relationship between the slave girl and master's son was completely forbidden. Still, Beau and Gloria blurred the lines.

Every school morning, Beau would be driven to school by an overseer. The sound of wagon wheels came barreling down the dirt road. The one horse carriage brought Beau home from school. This was the signal to Gloria. The slaves in the field shook their heads and murmured in disbelief as she ran out of the field. She ran to the backside of the main house, where the two would meet.

Beau took his hand-held chalkboard out of his satchel with Gloria at his side. He'd tell Gloria about his day at school. With his chalk and chalkboard in hand, Beau wrote and taught Gloria everything he learned in class. Gloria was like a sponge, taking in everything Beau showed her. Beau was a good teacher and friend. He even gave her an extra chalkboard with chalk so she could practice. Beau taught Gloria to read and write, which was against the rules. His mother had told him so. Beau ignored the rules because Gloria was his friend.

Beau favored Gloria. He gave her extra rations and made sure the overseers were not excessively hard on her. Beau's involvement with Gloria caused considerable controversy within the ranks of the slaves, and indignation to his mother. As a teenager, Beau began a courtship with Mae Stuart at the request and arrangement of his mother. She urged him to stop any relationship with the slave girl. To avoid any outward embarrassment, Beau distanced himself from Gloria after marrying Mae. The two would never be seen together openly.

Mae Jamison, Beau's wife, was a compliant, dutiful spouse. The former Mae (Stuart) was a socialite in her own right, with her father in the lumber industry when she married Beau Jamison. Mae quickly became a prominent figure in local Southern society, hosting some of the largest parties in the city.

Gloria realized that Beau had moved on with his marriage to Mae, so she decided to move on with her life as well. The Jamison plantation was about fifty acres large. Even with that swath of land around them, there was still not enough distance to stop the awkward glances between the two of them.

One hot August afternoon, Gloria and her best friend Beulah were in the cotton field. Gloria had just filled a burlap sack with cotton. She then tossed the sack onto the bed of the wagon. She pulled an empty sack from the front of the wagon and began her walk back to the field.

Removing the straw hat from her head, Beulah wiped the sweat from her brow and spoke. "You know that man on the roof has been looking at you all day."

Gloria replied, "Who you talking about?"

"You see that man standing on the roof," said Beulah.

Shaking her head, Gloria bent down to gather a handful of cotton from a cluster of plants and retorted, "I ain't paying that man no mind."

"You better, cause he's coming down the ladder," Beulah warned. "Gloria, fix yourself up! He's walking this way."

"Why is he coming this way?"

"I don't know, maybe he wants to get a closer look at you."

"How you know he's not coming for you?" Gloria laughed.

"Gloria, stop fooling around! That man is looking for you. Look at him! Tall, big muscles, and those pretty white teeth."

The man walked up in front of Gloria and Beulah and spoke, "Howdy, Ma'am," first to Beulah and then to Gloria. "My name is Mason, and I'm a carpenter on Master Beau's plantation. I've been working on the roof over there," he pointed to the barn. "I had to come down and see up close who that beautiful cotton picker was."

Gloria huffed, "You done seen me now. Now git!"

"Where's your manners?" Beulah's tone to her was reproachful.

Mason smiled, tipped his hat, then bid the two women "Adieu" as he walked away to finish his re-roofing project.

The next time Mason would see Gloria was at the harvest fest. Every October, the Jamison's had a fall holiday on their plantation for all their slaves. The festival was a celebration of the final harvested crops of the season. Beau was generous this year; he butchered two hogs. Everybody put on their best clothing. The women gorgeously wore their bonnets. There was food, music, dancing, and laughter everywhere. For a moment, a black man and a black woman could be free to forget he or she was a slave. Gloria was standing over near the punch bowl when Mason made his move. He walked over to her and began his conversation.

"Howdy, Ms. Gloria. It's good to see you again. I brought these flowers for you. They call them painted daisies."

Gloria took the flowers, then questioned suspiciously, "How do you know my name?"

"I made it my business to find out everything I could about you," Mason said.

"Oh, you have? Well, don't believe everything you hear."

Mason chuckled. "Everything I heard about you, you're a good woman with a kind heart."

Gloria smiled. She immediately turned her head, hoping that Mason had not seen her blush.

"That's the prettiest smile I ever seen." Mason was laying it on thick.

"Then you have been on Master Beau's roof way too long." Gloria turned and walked away, but Mason hurried to catch up and reached for her hand.

"Look here, Ms. Gloria. I knew I liked you the first time I looked at you from the roof of that old barn. And when I got close, I knew you were the girl for me."

"Is that so, Mr. Mason?" Gloria's brow scrunched in skepticism.

"Yes Ma'am, I believe so. I know this seems sudden, but I want to marry you, Ms. Gloria. If you say the same, I will love you and I promise to take care of you for the rest of my life. 'Course we must get Master Beau's approval first. So what say ya, Ms. Gloria?"

"I believe you be a fine man, Mr. Mason. The marrying kind – the kind most girls on the plantation would want to be hitched with. For me, I need to be sure that you be the right man for me."

"What I got to do to change your mind, Ms. Gloria?"

"Nothing, Mr. Mason. Everything in perfect time."

"Okay, Ms. Gloria, you win. I'll give you more time."

One morning, weeks after the festival, Gloria was driving the field wagon to the barn. She had driven the field wagon many times. This particular day as she drove the wagon through a patch of thorny sagebrush, unexpectedly one of the horses was spooked by a cottonmouth snake. The horses began to race uncontrollably, almost tipping over the wagon.

Gloria yelled, "Hold! Hold! Hold!"

The horses were out of control and were not obeying Gloria's command. Gloria continued to yell at the horses to hold, but to no avail. Unexpectedly, a silhouette of a man appeared against the backdrop of the morning sun. The tall muscular man looked at all the commotion and sprang into action. He sprinted across the field, singularly focused on stopping that runaway wagon. When he got close enough, he jumped onto the back of one of the horses and brought everything under control. That man was Mason.

Gloria sobbed, "Thank God you were here, Mason. I kept yelling at the horses, but they paid me no mind. Oh, Mason, I could've been a goner." Trembling, she fell into his arms.

"There, there, Ms. Gloria, it's alright now," he comforted her, wiping the tears from her eyes with a clean handkerchief from his overalls. "I love you, and I will always protect you, you got my word on that. I always want to be there for you every day, if you will have me."

"You really are a good man, a dependable man, Mr. Mason. I've had eyes for you for a long time, and I'd be honored to be your wife. Everything in perfect time."

Beau and the overseers were over at the scales inside the cotton barn checking the weight of that day's harvest. It was the end of the day and the field slaves turned in their equipment and headed home to the slave quarters. Up stepped Mason and Gloria to Beau.

Beau peered over his paperwork. "Gloria, Mason. What's on ya mind?"

Taking off his hat, Mason said, "Master Beau, me and Ms. Gloria want to get married."

"Well now, ain't that special. Is that so, Gloria?"

"Yes, Master Beau," Gloria bowed her head. "We want to get married."

Beau focused on Gloria. "Why? Haven't I been fairer to you than anybody? Didn't I always give you the biggest food ration? Didn't I always look after you? Is this how you pay me back?" Beau walked away, waving his hands and shaking his head.

Gloria ran after Beau and reached for his hand. They were now outside the barn.

"Since we were kids, you've been my best friend. You looked out for me like nobody else has." Gloria firmly held Beau's hand. "I can tell Ms. Mae makes you happy. I want to be happy too, Beau. Mason makes me happy."

Beau sighed. "Then go! Go ahead." With both disappointment and anger in his voice, he spoke forcibly. "You've got my permission!" Beau paused, thinking of how this situation could benefit himself, and turned back to Gloria. "I will give you my blessing under one condition. You, Mason, and any children must remain on the plantation as my property. You break this condition and I swear, I'll sell all of ya."

Reluctantly pursing her lips, Gloria replied, "We will obey everything you say, Master Beau."

Two Sundays later, Beau called all the slaves together under the large magnolia tree in front of the main house.

"Hey everybody, gather around. I got an announcement. I gave my blessing to Gloria and Mason to be married." Thunderous applause, hoots, and whistles of approval came from the attending slaves.

Beau continued on the steps of the main house, "Y'all step on up here now, Gloria and you too, Mason. We might as well do it today. I got a preacher. We might as well make it official." So it became legal and written in the Jamison slave journal that on October 14, 1844, Gloria and Mason were married.

The two spent their honeymoon night in a cabin Mason had built the previous spring near the forest. Mason worked as a carpenter fixing roofs and doing other carpentry projects around the plantation. He also worked at the new sawmill. With all the trees on his plantation, Beau had gone into the lumber business.

Nine months after their marriage, Gloria gave birth to a baby girl. Gloria named her Anna, after her mother. Two years later, Gloria delivered a baby boy. Mason named him Jupiter, after the planet, because of his size at birth. Mason said he was an enormous boy, as big as all outdoors. Two years later, Gloria gave birth to another baby girl. Gloria named her Joy, her mother's middle name. Two years passed and Gloria delivered a second boy. Gloria named him Caleb, after the Biblical Caleb, who brought a good report to Moses. Two years later, Gloria was pregnant again. This time, she and Mason would be blessed with a third baby girl. Mason named her Jennie. No special reason – he just liked the name.

One January afternoon, the sound of the sawmill filled the air. You could hear the giant saw ripping through trees, turning them into boards for construction. Mason always came home with a head full of sawdust. He loved it, saying it made him feel like he'd done a hard day's work. This particular Friday evening in January would turn the fortunes of this contented family upside down. Mason was late coming come home from work. Gloria figured he was tidying up at the mill. Master Beau trusted Mason so much that he made him the foreman. Word circulated about the slave quarters that there had been an accident at the sawmill. As more information leaked out, the fear was realized. There was indeed an accident. Mason had been killed.

Beau knocked on Mason and Gloria's cabin door.

Gloria removed her apron. "Master Beau, what brings you by?"

"Can I come in? I got something to tell you," he said, taking off his hat with one hand and covering his mouth with the other.

"Why are you looking so sad? Is something wrong? I've been waiting for Mason and his food is getting cold."

"Gloria, I need you to sit down. There was an accident at the mill. I'm not sure what happened, but Mason is dead."

Gloria screamed, "No! It can't be! What? How? No! This can't be." Weeping and wailing uncontrollably, Gloria fell to her knees. Young Anna and Jupiter walked into the room.

Anna placed her small hand on her mother's shoulder. "What's wrong Mommy? Why are you crying?"

Gloria mustered a coherent statement. "Your daddy has been in an accident and won't be coming home." Sobbing, heartbreak, and disbelief filled the little cabin.

Gloria, with her five children in tow, tearfully walked away from the freshly dug grave of Mason. After the funeral, Gloria and the children's lives would never be the same. In the evenings, as the orange sun set, sometimes in her mind she could visualize a tall silhouette of a man walking toward her. She'd smile and think, that's just Mason checking up on me and the kids. Gloria couldn't shake her sadness over losing him. The children struggled as well with their own sorrow. Gloria knew that she had to help her children by focusing on raising them. She decided the best way to honor her late husband was to not be a victim, and not let her children be victims, either. She poured her entire life into her children. She taught them to read and write as best she could. She taught them how to pray and the value of reading the Bible. Gloria instilled into her children tenacity and survival. She taught them about their past and inspired them to dream of a better future. It would be many years later before her children would unpack those golden nuggets of wisdom from their mother.

The following year's harvest was lean due to drought and the boll weevil. The food ration was sizably small for all the slaves, including Gloria and her youngsters, but somehow a crate full of food arrived at her door. Everybody knew it was from Beau.

Years went by and the older children, Anna, Jupiter, and Joy, joined Gloria in the field. Anna became quite a cotton picker. She could easily pick two hundred pounds of cotton a day. Meanwhile, the Civil War between the states had erupted, and to make matters worse, the drought destroyed much of the crops. Beau worried about how to keep the plantation going. He sold off several slaves, but he wouldn't touch Gloria or her children. In the spring of 1862, Gloria contracted typhoid fever. She would recover, but it left her vision impaired. Despite constant criticism from his wife Mae, Beau made it his business to check in on Gloria and the kids.

Anna, the eldest child, confided in her mother one evening after working the field that she was going to run away to the North that night. Gloria had known in her heart that someday she would have this conversation with one of her children, and somehow, she knew it would be the strong-willed Anna. Anna expressed that she wanted a better life for herself, her momma, and her siblings. She had acquired instructions from an abolitionist posing as a farmer on the way to town one day. The instructions outlined markers and contacts of those who would help her escape to freedom. She knew it would be dangerous, but freedom would be worth it. Anna packed her satchel with dry meats and fruit. She then took two canteens over to the well by the mulberry tree near the main house. She was hoping not to run into anyone. The evening was the time of day when slaves would go to well to fetch water for cooking. She made it to the well and filled up her canteen, and just as she turned, she saw Beau.

"Anna, what are you doing out here this late?"

"Uh," Anna improvised, "Momma needed water to cook some rice." She looked like she just seen a ghost.

"How is your momma doing?" Beau smirked, a toothpick hanging from his mouth.

Anna nodded, "Yes, yes, she's fine, sir."

"Tell your momma, if I have time this evening, I might stop by and look in on her." He looked up into the dark starry sky. "Beautiful night, ain't it?"

Anna replied nervously, "Yes sir, Master Beau, I'll tell her."

"Now you get on back to your place."

Anna told her momma that she had seen Master Beau, and he said he might come by later to visit her. She warned, "Careful, Momma. I don't trust that man. He can be generous at times, but at other times he can be mean as hell."

Gloria laughed, drawing Anna close to herself. "You leave Beau to me."

In spite of Anna's close encounter with Beau, she was still determined to run away. With her satchel and canteens filled, it was time to go.

Gloria called for the other children. "Jupiter, Joy, Caleb, and Jennie!" They all came running, hurrying to their mother's command.

Jupiter said, "What is it, Momma?"

"I need to tell you something. You have to be quiet about it. It is a secret! Nobody can know about what I'm about to tell you, not even Master Beau."

Joy echoed Jupiter, "What is it, Momma?"

Gloria sighed. "Anna is running away tonight."

Caleb exclaimed, "Is she crazy? Master Beau will lose his mind! Don't do it, Anna! Stay with us!"

"I know you're afraid, Caleb, but I must to do this. If we are to have any kind of future beyond this place, I have to do this for us. Look at me. I promise you, I'll be back for you."

Gloria gathered her children around her. "Let's pray. Heavenly Father, protect my baby. Keep her from harm. Give her wisdom and favor along this journey. Help her to make it to freedom. Amen."

After a round of hugs and tears, Gloria and her remaining sons and daughters sent Anna off.

Anna reminded her mother, "When I get to freedom and set up a place, I'm coming back for you, Momma. Jupiter, Joy, Caleb, and Jennie, I'm coming back for all of you, too."

Chapter 2
Anna Makes Her Move

Anna headed off into the dark, across the creek behind the slave quarters, into the tall trees.

The next morning, Master Beau was up early ringing the bell in front of the main house. The ringing of the bell meant the start of a new day. Master Beau was his regular sarcastic self, hurrying the slaves to the field.

Beau was saying, "Come on, come on. Y'all moving like a bunch of old ladies." Slave men, women, and children from all over the plantation came running. Among those he hastened to the field were Gloria, Jupiter, Joy, Caleb, and Jennie.

"I'm glad you and your young'uns could make it. I hope this bell wasn't too loud for you. Ha, ha," Beau laughed. "Hold everything. Wait just a gosh darn minute. Somebody is missing! Where the hell is Anna? I saw the little wench last night at the well getting water. She seemed a little nervous. She said you were making rice."

"I don't know where she is, Master Beau."

Beau responded, "There ain't but so many places she could be. Was she in the cabin when you and the other children left this morning?"

"No, I don't think so. I mean, I don't know, Master Beau."

By this time, Beau was getting angrier and his voice was getting louder.

He got within inches of her face. "Gloria, I'm going to ask you one more time, and don't you lie to me. Where the hell is Anna?" Yelling and cursing, Beau stomped away a few feet. He turned and walked back to Gloria, asking again as calmly as he could muster, "Where is Anna?"

Gloria responded, "I don't..." Before she could finish her sentence, Beau slapped her across her face. She fell to the ground, wincing in pain. In all her years knowing Beau, he had never struck her before. Jupiter was within hearing range of the altercation between his mother and Master Beau. It took four nearby slave men to restrain him. His anger burned in his chest, leaving him desperate to strike at Beau, but he was helpless to protect his mother.

Beau reminded Gloria of the threat he'd made to her and Mason before giving his blessing to their marriage. He swore that if Gloria or Mason broke the terms of the agreement, he'd sell everybody off.

Gloria responded as she got up off the ground. "I was wrong to bind my children to such a foolish agreement. It was the only way you would have allowed me and Mason to get married." Boldly she continued, "I don't know where Anna is, and if I knew, I wouldn't tell you anyway. You can do what you want with me, I'm old now. But my Anna, she deserves better."

Beau responded, "That little wench ran away, didn't she? Well, ain't that a kick in the teeth."

Beau motioned to a teen-age slave boy name Justin to come over to him. "Justin, I need you to ride ten miles to the Watson plantation and deliver this note to Master Jim Watson." He hurriedly scrawled on a piece of paper.

> **I need the services of the Railroad men immediately. My prized cotton picker ran away. She goes by the name of Anna. She is 19 years old, about 5 feet 3 inches, about 100 lbs. soaking wet. She has a scar on her right hand from a cooking accident. I want a warrant put out for her capture and return. She is a valuable slave, so bring her back with no damage or harm and I will pay five hundred dollars.**
>
> **Signed,**
> **Beau Jamison**

During the day, Anna stayed in the cover of trees. That was when she rested and ate. At night, she pushed forward, staying close to the river, which was always to her left. She occasionally daydreamed about her momma and her siblings. She wondered what they would be doing that time of day. Jupiter had the biggest laugh ever. His voice was so deep that it always filled the cabin, the fields, wherever he was. Joy was an excellent cook and seamstress. She made the best biscuits, with butter and honey. Caleb loved animals. One day he nursed an injured baby bird back to health. Jennie was the smart one; Momma taught her to read and write before she was five years old. She took a moment to relax and read a book of adventures by Mark Twain. Reading always brought comfort to Anna. It allowed her to escape the tediousness of slave work. The sun was setting. Soon it would be nightfall, which meant she needed to move. The instructions told her to look for the marker of a gigantic rock with an X on it. The markers assured her that she was headed in the right direction. Even under the starry skies of darkness, the glow of the moon seemed to light her way. After passing the huge rock with an X, the next marker was a corn field. The instructions said to keep the corn field to her right and the river to her left. Anna traveled all evening, stopping only to refill her canteens. Soon it would be daybreak. Anna figured after being gone three days, Master Beau, or worse, the slave catchers, would be looking for her. It was now daylight and Anna rested in the corn field. Just as she closed her eyes, she heard voices. She turned to get a better view, and spotted two men on a dirt road with horses. Neither of the men looked like Master Beau. Perhaps Master Beau had hired two slave catchers. Soon the men rode off. Anna was now alone in the corn field. After spending the entire day in the corn field, night was quickly approaching, and that meant she needed to press on toward the next marker. Keenly she detected the sound of horses. Had those two men returned, or were these different men? She heard someone call out her name.

One of the men yelled, "Anna, I know you're out there somewhere. Give up and all will be forgiven."

The other man climbed off his horse and yelled into the darkness, "Come on, Anna. Master Beau misses you. Your momma has been crying for you. There is no reason for you to be out here. It is not safe out here. Nobody will harm you, so come out."

The man on the horse said to the one who had dismounted, "She's not coming out. This one is not going to be easy."

The man who dismounted his horse reminded his partner, "Remember what Beau said: Don't hurt or damage the girl. Oh, what the hell, enough of this nonsense! Send in the dogs."

Almost immediately, Anna heard the sound of hounds in the distance. Should she run or stay hidden? The sound of horses and dogs seemed to be getting closer. Her decision was made for her, and she ran. As the dogs and the two who rode the horses tore through the corn field, Anna ran as fast as she could. The terror from the barking dogs and the galloping horses was emotionally overwhelming. Anna's heart was beating so fast it felt as if it would explode in her chest.

With the river to her left and the corn field to her right, Anna remembered something her little brother Caleb taught her about dogs. Caleb informed her one evening as they sat on the back porch that dogs cannot track through water. If she crossed the river, the howling dogs would lose her scent.

Without hesitation, Anna raced into the river. The water was frigid cold! It felt like a thousand bees stinging her, but she kept moving against the rushing current. Exhausted, she finally crossed to the other side of the river and collapsed onto the outer bank. The sound of dogs began to fade into the night as the hounds lost her scent. Anna gathered herself, catching her breath. She laughed and cried at such a close call. She couldn't believe a conversation with Caleb had been so valuable.

"Thank you, little brother. You saved my life."

She continued her walk toward her next marker. The next landmark would be a church. She wondered who would put a place of worship out here, in the middle of nowhere.

Anna had been walking for hours and was getting tired. Crossing the river had taken much of her strength. The terrain was very hilly, and she looked for a place to rest for the night, out of plain sight. Just as she had determined she had gone as far as she could go for the night, Anna saw a glow in the distance. *Could that be the church?* she thought to herself. The lantern on the porch was a beacon of hope, like the smile of her best friend Beulah. Immediately, Anna got a burst of energy. The closer she got to that beautiful light, the more her tired legs and feet seemed energized. At the front door, she knocked and then pounded the door again, but nobody answered. She continued to beat on the door, ignoring the dull ache developing on the side of her fist. Finally, she saw a figure with a lantern through the stained-glass window.

"What do you want?" came a voice from the opposite side of the door.

Anna responded, "I came a long way, and I need your help."

An older black man cracked the door slightly and asked, "How can I help you, young lady?"

"My name is Anna Jamison, and I was told to ask for Minister Smalls, and he would help me."

The older man behind the door said, "I'm Reverend Walter Smalls."

As the door opened wider, tears of joy filled her eyes. Anna held on to Minister Smalls tightly. Her grip was like that of a drowning person to a life boat. The reverend's embrace was a welcome relief. It was a great comfort for Anna to finally relax.

Reverend Smalls hollered for his wife. "Janie! Oh, Janie!!"

"What is it, Walter? What could be so important this time of night?"

"I want you to meet Anna. She has come a long way. Can you get her something to eat and some clean dry clothes?"

Janie sized Anna up. "Let me look at you. I think I have some clothing that will fit you just fine."

Grateful, Anna replied, "Thank you, Minister Smalls, and you too, Ms. Janie."

Janie smiled graciously. "Child, you are welcome. You are not far from crossing that bridge to freedom."

Curiously, Anna asked, "If you are so close to freedom, why do you stay here?"

Janie responded, "The Reverend and me are free people. We serve the Lord by helping our people get to freedom. It is dangerous business, and those pesky Railroad men are always trying to find out something. Thanks be to God, he has kept us safe."

Reverend Smalls interrupted. "Anna, I need to acquaint you with some people. You will be traveling tomorrow evening with this group. You are less than twenty miles from freedom. The man who will be leading this party has made this trip many times. His name is Obadiah."

Reverend Smalls walked to the center of the kitchen and pushed the large wooden table away. He rolled up a throw rug to expose a trap door to the basement. Lifting up the door, he climbed down the ladder. Anna followed the Reverend to the cellar.

"Howdy, Reverend," Obadiah spoke.

"Hello, Obadiah. I want to introduce you and the rest of the party to Anna. She will be traveling with you tomorrow to freedom."

Obadiah stretched out his right hand to Anna. "Don't you worry none, Ms. Anna. Everything is gonna be alright. By the way, everybody calls me O.B."

The next day, Ms. Janie fixed a huge breakfast. Anna had never seen so many flapjacks, piles of bacon, and potatoes. The traveling party ate until everyone was stuffed. The travelers would still be full from the huge breakfast meal when evening came.

Reverend Smalls yelled from upstairs, "The coast is clear! Hurry, it is time to go."

The group hugged the Reverend and Ms. Janie. Everybody expressed their appreciation for the love, protection, and hospitality from this lovely couple at a church in the middle of nowhere.

As the new band of travelers disappeared beyond the huge sycamore tree, O.B. had one final instruction. "We must all stay together. We all get to freedom, or none of us."

The Railroad men were always out in the evening trying to catch an unsuspecting slave not paying attention. O.B. was a great leader. He kept everybody's spirits up. The twenty-mile journey went quickly. *It's relaxing to travel with companions*, Anna thought to herself. It was a major relief not to have to think of every detail. She and her fellow travelers were almost free.

O.B. said, "Look everyone! See that tall white house on the hilltop? That house belongs to Mr. Willingham. He is a friend of the slave. He told me that he put his house on that great big hill so those who needed help could find it. Now all we have to do is cross the bridge, climb that hill, knock on the basement door, and we will be free."

The group quietly crossed the bridge, climbed the steep hill, and knocked on the basement door. The door opened slowly, then an elderly white man carrying a lantern welcomed the weary travelers into his home.

"Welcome everyone, my name is Albert Willingham and this is my wife Roberta. I call her Bertie.'"

Roberta spoke. "We've been expecting you all. Come upstairs, I have made dinner for you. Y'all rest up after you eat. Tomorrow we will get each of you your freedom document and a new name, if you want one."

Anna liked her name. It was given to her by her momma, and she was keeping it. The freedom paper was what she really coveted. She couldn't think of anything more precious than to have her name on that paper. Anna Jamison, the former slave, now the emancipated woman.

The next day, Ms. Bertie took the entire company of travelers over to the newspaper building to acquire their liberation papers. On the streets were people who looked like them, walking freely, with not a care in the world. She took the group of people to the back room where a man had a printing press. The man asked their names, where they came from, and ages. He recorded this information in a book he kept under his desk. When the man got to Anna, he asked what name she wanted on her free paper. She proudly said, "Anna Jamison!"

It had been a month since Anna received her freedom. She was now working as a domestic for the Governor during the week, and a cook at a local restaurant on the weekend. She rented a room at the local Mission. Anna's goal was to purchase a storefront building she passed every day on her way to work. The shop had two rooms and a kitchen upstairs. The wide-open space downstairs was perfect for a store. Anna said to herself, "This will be mine one day."

"Momma would be so proud of me." Anna beamed with confidence as she headed off to the Governor's mansion.

Now, it had been a year since Anna was given her freedom. Anna saved enough money to acquire the shop she had her eye on. The owner of the building was a Mr. Samuel Jenkins, a butcher at the local meat market. Mr. Jenkins was a good friend of Mr. Willingham. Mr. Willingham heard about Anna's work ethic and vouched for her. Mr. Samuel Jenkins shook Anna's hand and sold her the facility.

Anna moved out of her one room at the Mission into her newly purchased store front dwelling. Even with her new-found success, Anna was still discontent. She missed her momma and her siblings.

Chapter 3
I Must Go Back

One summer evening, Anna paid a visit to the Willingham home. She knocked on the door.

"Anna, come in," said Bertie. "It has been a long time! How have you been?"

Anna responded, "I've been fine. Things are going well, only..."

"Only what, child?"

"I want my family with me. I want my momma, my brothers, and my sisters with me. Freedom doesn't feel like freedom without my kinfolks."

"So, what do you want to do?"

"I want to go back to the plantation and bring my people back with me."

Bertie sighed. "I was afraid you were going to say that. You know that getting here was dangerous enough, but going back is suicide. However, I do understand."

"Please tell Mr. Albert not to be mad at me. If I'm not back in two weeks, then I didn't make it. But I have got to try to bring my family back. I'll be leaving tomorrow."

Anna packed a satchel with food along with her freedom papers. Before departing town, she filled two canteens with water at the Willingham well. The Willinghams prayed with Anna, then hugged her and bid her farewell.

Albert smiled grimly. "We'll be looking for your return, Anna. God speed."

Anna walked away without turning back, not wanting the Willinghams to see the tears in her eyes. She continued down the hill and across the bridge and then out of sight. The journey back to the Jamison plantation had begun.

The strategy for going back would be slightly different from when she came. She knew that leaving the plantation, the river was on the left and the corn field was on the right. Going back, the corn field was on the left and the river stayed on the right. The markers were there to point her in the right direction. One thing that did not change: she traveled at night and rested during the day.

Returning, Anna seemed to make better time. It wasn't long before she passed the church sitting in the midst of nowhere. She considered a brief stop to visit Reverend and Ms. Janie Smalls, but decided she needed to stay focused, so she pushed on. Anna remembered how kind the Smalls were. Those flapjacks Ms. Janie made would hold you for an entire day.

On the third day, Anna was awakened by the sound of barking dogs. Anna hoped that she could avoid any contact with the Railroad men. Being stopped by the professional slave catchers meant trouble. From a distance, she noticed a black man running. It looked like the Railroad men and their hounds were hot on his trail. Anna felt sorry for him.

His situation had gone from bad to worse. Which was worse – being hunted down by the slave catchers with growling, vicious dogs, or facing an angry master?

On the fourth day, Anna began to notice familiar scenery. She was less than a day's walk to Beau Jamison's plantation. Anna hid during the day in the corn field. The corn stocks were waist-high, which made for excellent covering. From her vantage point, she could view slaves walking on a dirt road. Anna maintained her silence, definitely not wanting to draw any attention. Soon it would be nightfall, and she would begin her final push to rescue her momma and siblings.

On the fifth night, Anna reached the Jamison plantation. The spectacle of fireworks going off everywhere provided the perfect distraction for Anna to sneak into the slave quarters, particularly her momma's cabin.

"Anna, is that you?" Anna's mother, Gloria, gasped. "Lordy, I can't believe it's you! My baby, you came back. Come closer. I don't see that well now. I just wanna hold your face with my hands."

"Momma, I came back for you. I came back to take you away from this awful place." "Where are Jupiter, Caleb, Joy, and Jennie?"

"They are coming. Everybody has been talking about you all day. They say you been hiding out in the corn field."

"Yes, Momma, but I'm here now."

Abruptly, the door opened. In walked Jupiter, Caleb, Joy, and Jennie. The tiny cabin was filled with smiles, pearly white teeth, and laughter.

Gloria cautioned, "Y'all be quiet! Y'all know Master Beau can hear a mouse pee on cotton, even with all this firework noise."

Jupiter jubilantly spoke up. "We know, Momma. We just so happy to see Anna."

Joy peppered her with questions. "Where you been? Was you really free? Is everything prettier up North? I've been told it was."

The youngest, Caleb and Jennie, listened breathlessly to hear what stories Anna would tell about her adventures up North.

Anna urgently spoke. "I'll tell you everything you need to know, but right now we have got to go! We don't have much time." Anna paused and then gave them a glimpse of what awaited them. "Freedom makes you feel fresh and clean, like drinking cool water after working the field all day. Happiness, life, dreams are in your hands, not the Master's."

Joy anxiously spoke up. "Momma, you coming with us?"

"No, child, this is where I belong."

Jupiter retorted, "If you don't go, we're not going."

Gloria said, "Listen to me, everybody. I've been on Mr. Beau's plantation for over forty years now, and it has been fair some days, but mostly hard." She paused, then continued, "I used to think about finding my family, but those days are long gone. It's your time now."

Jennie gasped, "But, Momma!"

Gloria interrupted, "I want my babies to taste the cool waters of freedom like Anna said. Your life is ahead of you in the free world. The best of my life is behind me. I'll be alright. I remember the wonderful life I had with your father on this plantation. I've also seen a lot of sad things in this place. One day this life as a slave will be over for me. On that great day, me and Mason will be together again, in heaven."

Gloria shook her head and said resolutely, "Now, mind me. I want y'all to listen to Anna. She knows what she is doing. She knows the way. No back talk! Obey her like you would listen to me. Do you hear what I say?"

In a chorus together they replied, "Yes, Momma."

"I fixed y'all some food for your journey. I put some hardtack bread, salted meats, beans, flour, corn meal, and six canteens full of water. Jupiter, you my big boy, look out for your family."

Each said their tearful goodbye, somehow knowing in their heart that this would be the last they would see of their momma.

The five Jamison children - Anna, Jupiter, Joy, Jennie, and Caleb - began their journey to freedom.

As they walked, Anna pointed up. "Y'all see that full moon? It's going to light our way to independence." She continued, "We will do most of our traveling at night, 'cause the night will cover us from the slave catchers. We will rest, eat, and remain hidden in the trees or corn fields during the day. The corn stocks are high this time of year, so it should provide cover for our safety. We must stay together and move quickly. When I say go, I mean move now!"

After a moment, she added, "Keep an eye out for the Railroad men, y'all hear me?"

They all said together, "We hear you, Anna, we hear ya."

The Railroad men were always out on patrol trying to catch runaway slaves. These men were paid professional slave catchers hired by vindictive owners to capture and return runaways to their masters. Tragically, an unsuspecting runaway sometimes followed the railroad tracks to escape to freedom. Unfortunately for the slave, the railroad tracks were heavily patrolled. These hired slave catchers were often accompanied by dogs to help them hunt down runaways. These men are heartless beasts. They are paid to show no mercy to a runaway.

Chapter 4

Rob, Claire, Benji, And Lucy's Big Adventure

$\mathcal{I}$t has been barely two weeks since the end of the school year. The eagerly awaited summer vacation is finally here, and the children of William and Audrey James are already feeling the effects of nothing to do. The faded memories of homework, getting up early, and cafeteria food have given way to shear boredom.

William James, a lieutenant at the local Willingham fire station, grabs a cup of coffee and kisses his wife, Audrey, goodbye as he heads off to work. The smell of bacon fills the house as mom toasts the bread for her signature bacon-cheese sandwich.

"I'm bored!" proclaims Claire. "There is nothing to eat. I've got nothing to wear. Let's go to the mall and have our nails done," she says to her best friend, Nell.

Mom speaks up. "Claire, get off that phone and clean your room. It looks like a pig pen."

Claire's brother Rob interjects, "Yeah, Claire, your room smells like B.O.!"

Claire retorts, "Shut up, Rob! Nobody's talking to you."

Their mother asks, "Where is Benji?"

Rob scoffs while checking his latest social media post, "You know that little nerd, he's been downstairs playing video games all morning."

"Stop talking about your little brother like that. Brunch is ready! Claire, I told you to get off that phone."

"Mom, can you drop me off at the mall? Nell and I are going to get manicures."

"You and Nell need to do something about your unibrows. You both look like Anthony Davis," Rob guffaws.

"Rob! When did you get to be so mean?" The reprimand comes sternly from his mother.

"Sorry, Mom, I was just playing."

Benji, who'd appeared from the basement and is already stuffing his face, chirps with his mouth full, "This is the best bacon-cheese sandwich I have ever had! You're the best, Mom!"

Lucy barks her agreement.

Benji continues, "See, Mom! Lucy likes your bacon-cheese sandwich too."

Claire rolls her eyes. "What a kiss-up."

"Claire! You're as bad as Rob, and no, I'm not taking you to the mall. I have a surprise for the three of you."

They all politely ask in harmony, "What is it? What is it, Mother?"

Benji asks excitedly, "Are we getting a cat?"

"Ugh, I hope not, I'm not taking care of anymore animals," Rob grunts.

"No, we are not getting a cat. We are going to the new library."

Claire and Rob moan. "What? No, Mom, no! Who goes to the library?"

Benji eagerly shoves the last bite of his sandwich into his mouth. "Me and Lucy will go to the library!"

Rob snarls, "Shut up, loser."

"Hey, that's enough of that. The library and the Freedom Bridge are having a Grand Opening today. I think it will be educational for all three of you."

Mom reads the brochure about the new library that came in the mail yesterday. She shares the interesting facts about the new library and bridge.

The new library is built over the home of abolitionists Albert and Roberta Willingham.

The Willingham home was destroyed by fires three times and was rebuilt twice.

The Freedom Bridge dedication marked the crossing from slavery to freedom.

The Freedom Bridge originally had no name.

The original bridge was a narrow rickety wooden structure.

Rob's only comment is, "I heard that there are some basketball courts near the library. Can I bring my basketball?" He bounces his ball on the kitchen floor.

Mom answers, "All right, now can we all get in the car?"

Claire sighs as she climbs into the front passenger seat and stares out the window. "This is so lame."

"Mom, can Lucy come? Please?" Benji never likes to leave Lucy behind.

"Fine. Perhaps we can pass her off as a support dog. Now can we just go?"

Mom and the kids drive into the library's parking lot. Ribbons and balloons are tied to the front entrance. As Mom, the kids, and Lucy walk through the door, they are greeted with a "thank you for coming" and a smile from the librarian. Everybody except Lucy; she is greeted with frowns and whispers from the patrons.

Ms. Rebekah Peters, the librarian, confronts Audrey. "Uh, Ma'am, you can't bring that dog in here."

Audrey replies, "It's all right. She is our support dog."

Mr. Jessie Washington, Ms. Peters assistant, grits his teeth as Lucy walks past him. His twisted lips and arched eyebrow are funny to the kids.

Ms. Peters asks, "Would anyone like a tour of our new facility? I would love to show you around."

Lucy woofs, wagging her tail, totally ignoring Mr. Washington's expression.

Mr. Washington snarls again. Under his breath, he mutters, "Kids!" as he walks with his cart behind the tour.

Audrey instructs, "Kids, introduce yourselves."

First Claire, then Rob, then lastly Benji say their names. Benji adds, "This is Lucy."

Lucy barks.

As Ms. Peters shows the James family all the new areas of the library, she stops to highlight the new computer room and mentions the free Wi-Fi. As the tour continues, Ms. Peters tells about the historical beginnings of the library. She notes everything on the brochure, including that the library was built over the house of Albert and Roberta Willingham, who were abolitionists.

Benji asks, "What is an ab-ol-i-tion-ist?"

Ms. Peters responds, "That is an excellent question. Abolitionists were men and women alike who opposed people being use as slaves. You must understand, our country was split along the lines of some states that were for slavery, and others against. The abolitionists, at great risk to themselves, helped runaway slaves to freedom."

Rob asks, "Is that why we're honoring the bridge?"

"Another wonderful question! The bridge we're observing is not just any bridge. The Freedom Bridge was a passage from oppression and slavery to a life of liberty and freedom."

Not wanting to be outdone by her brothers, Claire chimes in. "Why would somebody buy and sell another human being? That's just wrong."

"You kids ask great questions. Slavery was a system. People of color had to be dehumanized for the system to work. Once you dehumanize a group of people, they become like a tool or equipment, not human beings. Their masters could torture and brainwash them and tell them they were inferior. Sadly, there was no to one defend them. The slaves were at the mercy of their owners. Not all slaves were passive. Some risked everything in pursuit of freedom, and some sacrificed their lives. And not all slave masters were the same. Some were very harsh; others allowed a limited amount of independence. But, at the end of the day, a slave was property; they belonged to someone else."

Audrey interrupts, "I just received a call from the garage repairman. Will it be all right to leave the kids here for a little while?"

Ms. Peters looks at Mr. Washington. He shoots back, "Don't look at me. I ain't no babysitter."

Ms. Peters nods. "Sure. We're not that busy, and we have plenty to keep them busy."

"Thank you very much. I'll be back as soon as I can." Audrey hurries out with a grateful smile and a stern admonishment to her children to behave.

Mr. Washington suggests to Ms. Peters, "Do you want me to show them the old door to the cellar?"

"I don't know, Mr. Washington. It's been quite a while since anyone has been down there."

Benji's interest is already piqued. "I want to see the basement! Can I? Can I see it, please?"

Jessie Washington leads the children to the back of the library where there is an old wooden door. With a twinkle in his eyes, he reaches to the ledge above the door for an old brass skeleton key tied with a faded purple ribbon. Slowly he unlocks the door to the dark basement. He tells them the light switch is over against the wall beside the copy machine. One by one, the children proceed down the steps.

Claire makes a face, sweeping away cobwebs with her hands. "Disgusting! I hate spiderwebs and bugs, and where is the light switch?"

"What are you afraid of? I see a spider making a nest in your hair," Rob teases.

"Stop it, Rob! I hate dark basements. They give me the creeps!"

Benji attempts to reassure his sister. "Come on, Claire, I'll hold your hand. Don't forget, we have Lucy, the wonder dog."

With a shiver, Claire follows. "Fine, I'll go. But the first creepy thing that happens, I'm so out of here."

From the top step, Mr. Washington reminds the children before shutting the door, "When you want to come back, just knock on the door." Just as Claire, Rob, Benji, and Lucy reach the bottom of the stairs, an intense bright light from the copy machine accompanied by an intense swirling wind surrounds all three of them.

"What is happening?" Claire shouts anxiously.

Rob looks around. "I don't know, but my hands and my face feel funny."

"Wow, this is so super amazing!" Benji is fearless, as always.

Lucy is now barking repeatedly.

Suddenly, the three are in complete darkness. As their eyes adjust, their vision fades from shades of black to gray. Trees from a forest cast an eerie shadow. Except for the brilliance of the moon, nothing looks familiar. The portal in the basement has left the three children and Lucy in a wooded forest. *Where were they? How did they get here?* The sounds of the night surround them. Owl screeches, cricket chirps, and frog croaks fill the air. The rustling of forest animals makes the scene even more terrifying.

"Okay, everybody stay calm," says Rob. "There has got to be a logical explanation. What it is, I don't know."

Claire whispers, "I'm scared, Rob. I want to go home. Where is that stupid door?"

Benji nervously responds, "I'm afraid too, but maybe we are here for a reason."

Claire retorts, "What possible explanation could that be? *Smart butt!*"

"I don't know the exact reason, but last summer our scout leader told us that if we were ever lost, we should look for the North star, listen for a river, keep an open ear for people talking, but most importantly, travel in the open space."

"Sounds good to me, little brother," Rob shrugs. "Let's stay close to the forest, but not in the forest."

Claire takes out her cell phone. "I'm calling Mom. Darn, I have no bars on my phone. The reception really sucks out here."

The three kids and Lucy walk for what seems like an hour. The moon, the stars, and the night creatures accompany them.

Startled, Rob pauses. "Do you hear that?"

"Hear what?" Claire stops behind him.

"It's the sound of rushing water. Could it be a river?"

Benji chimes in. "I hear it, too! At least we'll have something to drink."

Claire quickly speaks, "I'm not drinking or eating anything out here."

Lucy, however, doesn't hesitate to run to the river and lap up the cool water.

Benji and Rob follow Lucy. They cup their hands and drink from the refreshing river. Claire stands back, not having anything to do with her brothers and that crazy dog.

Claire pulls out her phone again. "I can't believe this stupid phone. Wait! I hear something. Everybody shut up!"

Lucy barks excessively.

Benji follows her gaze. "What is it, girl?" Lucy turns toward the forest and barks repeatedly. In a split-second, she dashes into the forest. Benji and Rob call her name, but she's gone.

Frustrated, Rob stands with his arms cross. "Where is that dog?" For the first time, Benji is upset. He wails, "I think she's lost! We've got to find her!"

Claire is moved by seeing her little brother cry. Although she was never a big fan of Lucy's, she knows the love Benji has for his dog.

"It's going to be all right, little brother. We will find Lucy, I promise." Pulling Benji close to herself, she gives him a hug, wiping his tears away with her hand.

Rob says, "Claire, you sound like Mom. That was a good thing you did. Let's see if we can find that dog."

The three go into the night, calling for Lucy.

"Where is that dog?" Rob asks again.

As swiftly as she had darted into the forest, Lucy quickly sprints out several feet in front of the three, again barking.

Benji says, "I see her! She is right up there." He runs ahead, leaving his brother and sister behind. When Benji reaches her, he kneels down and hugs Lucy's neck. She licks his face in return. When Rob and Claire catch up, they too give Lucy hugs. Suddenly, Lucy breaks away from the celebration, walks over to the edge of the forest, and starts barking again.

Benji tugs on his brother's arm. "I think she's saying something. I think she wants us to follow her."

Claire is skeptical. "Are you serious? You think we should go back into the forest?"

"Yeah. Lucy is my best friend, and I trust her," Benji pleads.

Rob tentatively agrees. "I'm not sure, but let's see. Maybe Lucy can help us find our way out of here."

"Fine, let's follow the dog. Does anybody think that following a dog in the dark is a bad idea?" Claire's grumbles are reluctant at best.

The three follow Lucy through the thick foliage of the forest. Lucy periodically turns around to bark to ensure her followers stay behind her. Suddenly, Lucy stops in her tracks. The kids catch up with her.

"Now what?" says Claire.

The forest seems extremely quiet - no hooting owls, no sound of crickets, just silence. The darkness has an eerie sound of its own.

Claire whispers, "I hear something."

Lucy barks.

Rob agrees. "I hear something, as well. I hear voices. Who are they? The footsteps are getting closer."

The three huddle closer to each other, afraid, scared of who would come out of the darkness.

Lucy barks again.

Chapter 5

Courage
And
Heroes

*B*enji implores Lucy to be quiet. The voices and footsteps stop and there again is that eerie feeling of darkness. A voice out of the blackness speaks, "There's that dog!"

"Come here, dog," a man's voice calls.

Afraid and shaking, Claire, Rob, and Benji pack in even closer.

The man questions, "Who are you? What y'all doing out here?" The man and four others come into view.

A woman now asks the questions. "What is your name? What y'all doing out here? Are y'all friendly to slaves?"

Fearfully, Claire stammers. "We, we, we are lost. We don't even understand how we got here. This is my brother Rob, I'm Claire, and this is my little brother Benji. We are just trying to find our way home."

"Well, Miss Claire," the woman detects an obviously anxious moment. "Those are some strange duds y'all wearing." Focusing on the 21st century attire worn by the

James kids, she continues. "Never saw this kind of clothing on anyone, not even on the rich southern socialites."

"My name is Anna, Anna Jamison," the woman introduces herself. "This big fella is my brother Jupiter."

"Howdy, Ma'am," Jupiter speaks to Claire.

Anna continues, "These two are my sisters, Joy and Jennie, and my baby brother Caleb."

"Howdy, Ma'am," they politely say.

Anna resumes, "Y'all are welcome to travel with us."

Rob asks, "Where are you going?"

"To freedom, God willing. If we're lucky, to Mr. Willingham's house."

"What? What are you saying? Who's Mr. Willingham?" Rob's questions fly out of his nervous mouth.

"Y'all can stay out here by yourselves if you want to, but I wouldn't recommend it. It's unsafe out here for people who look like us."

Claire, Rob, and Benji all nod in harmony. "We're going with you."

Anna gives important instructions to Claire, Rob, and Benji before they leave. She warns them about the Railroad men. She informs them that these men are dangerous hired slave catchers. Anna tells them they must stick together and obey her voice. She explains to them that there are markers along the way to point them in the right direction. Anna instructs them that they will travel at night under the cover of darkness and rest during the day among the trees or in the corn fields. Anna concludes, "The river must always be to your left hand and the corn field to your right hand."

Claire speaks to Anna, "Hey girl, your duds look pretty strange to me also. I guess style is not your thing."

Anna, Joy, and Jennie go silent, not knowing how to take what Claire has said. But suddenly, they burst out with laughter. Joy shakes her head and slaps her leg. "I've told Anna over and over that she dresses like an old lady."

Again, the laughter bursts out, causing Jupiter to ask, "What are y'all laughing about?"

Joy giggles again, "Just women stuff."

Jennie joins her, "Yea, women stuff. You wouldn't understand."

Jupiter scoffs, "Jennie, you ain't nowhere close to being a woman."

Jennie challenges him, "I'm almost twelve years old, and I can out-wrestle and out-run most boys my age."

Unsure how to ask, Rob ventures, "This might seem like a stupid question, but what year is it to you?"

Joy rolls her eyes. "That was an empty-headed question. Everybody knows it is July 4, 1864."

"What?" Rob, Claire, and Benji together exclaim.

Claire moans, "This can't be happening. This is a nightmare."

Benji pinches Claire. "Seems pretty real to me."

Claire jerks away from him. "Stop it, you little rodent."

Caleb brings the conversation back around. "If it is not July 4, 1864, then what year and date is it to you, Rob?"

"It is July 4, 2020. My dad and I were going to grill out later today."

"What the Sam Hill is going on?" Jupiter stops in shock.

"Hold on, everybody," says Benji, analyzing the situation and giving his best guess. "I think my sister, my brother, Lucy, and I have become time travelers. We entered a time portal in the basement of the library, and suddenly here we are in 1864."

"What! What are you talking about?" Claire can't believe what she is hearing.

"Think about it, Claire," Rob interjects. "What Benji says makes sense. How else can you explain how we got here?"

Anna, Jupiter, Joy, Caleb, and Jennie keep quiet while listening to their three new friends come to grips with the possibility of time travel. The five of them are equally confused as to how this could happen.

Anna finally speaks up. "I don't care how this happened, or why, but our plans have not changed. Maybe we will figure this out along the way, but for now we need to keep moving to our next marker, which is the gigantic rock with an X on it."

The first evening, the eight travelers get acquainted. Although 19th century people and 21st century people are light years apart in many ways, freedom, family, and home are something both groups have in common.

Anna, Joy, and Jennie bond with Claire almost immediately, talking about girl stuff in the 19th century versus girl stuff in the 21st century. Jupiter and Caleb talk about what life on the plantation had been like. Rob and Benji share what their modern life with phones and computers is like. Rob and Benji can't relate to how hard Jupiter and Caleb worked, especially for not being paid. Jupiter tells Rob about the physical punishment he received for talking back and not doing his chores. Rob tells Jupiter that talking back and not doing his chores cost him a week's allowance. Jupiter and Caleb can hardly understand this thing called technology and how it would change everything. They also can't believe how much free time Rob and Benji have.

The eight finally reach the gigantic rock with an X on it. Anna suggests that everyone rest. The morning sunrise is on the horizon, so each person rests in the corn field. While Claire,

Rob, and Benji struggle to get comfortable, Anna, Jupiter, Joy, Caleb, and Jennie make the best of the situation. Lucy doesn't seem to mind the corn field as long as Benji is near.

While everyone sleeps, there is an unusual stirring in corn field. The rustling is the sound of footsteps, like soldiers marching. In the distance is the sound of exploding cannons and gun fire.

Anna says, "Everybody get up and head toward the river."

Anna and the group get up and run toward and across the river. The marching army is the Confederate soldiers passing less than 100 feet from where the travelers had been sleeping. The eight barely escape the advancing rebel military. They run to the nearest hill to take refuge in an apple orchard.

Anna asks breathlessly, "Is everybody safe?"

"Yes, I think so," Rob answers, catching his breath from the steep climb. "No, wait! Where is Jennie?"

Jennie has stopped her ascent up the hill. She has become paralyzed by the smoke, gunfire, and explosions. There she is, kneeling behind a bush with her hands covering her ears. Rob sees her from his position.

Rob yells to Anna above the noise, "I see her. I have got to help her." He clasps his ears with both hands from a nearby explosion.

Before Anna can respond, Rob races down the hill, covering his face from the debris of cannon fire. When he finally reaches Jennie, he covers her with his body as they both hide behind the bush.

What they are now witnessing is a Civil War battle. In a clearing just below the tree line, the two armies face off. Fire and smoke erupt. The sound of bugles on each side blares. Someone yells, "Charge!" and then the hand-to-hand combat begins. The fighting only lasts about thirty minutes before one bugler blows the retreat from the Confederate side. The soldiers in blue celebrate with a cheer as the soldiers in gray retreat from the battlefield. After the battle, Jennie and Rob reemerge from hovering behind the bush and rejoin the other six travelers.

Anna tells Rob, "That was a brave thing you did. Thank you for saving my little sister."

Jupiter, Joy, Caleb, Claire, and Benji all join the chorus of thanking Rob for his bravery. Benji says to Rob, "That was the coolest thing I ever saw you do." He then gives Rob a thumbs up.

Jupiter asks Anna, "You think we should join ourselves with the soldiers in blue?"

Anna sternly speaks, "No, Jupiter. They mind their business, we mind ours."

Jupiter argues, "The soldiers in blue, they be friendly towards slaves."

Anna becomes angry. "Jupiter, you listen to me. We can't trust anybody, not even the soldiers in blue. We will get to freedom together, or not at all. You hear me?"

"I hear ya, Anna. Sorry," Jupiter nods.

Anna says in a softer voice to her big brother, "We still have a long way to go. I need you, we all need you. We must stick to the plan."

The eight wait in the apple orchard until sunset. The burning smell of cannon fire gives way to the pleasant smell from the apple trees. An added benefit is the golden delicious apples. The tasty fruit makes for a great snack.

Night has fallen, and Anna rouses herself and speaks to the group. "Get up, it's time to go. The next marker is two days away. This is one of the most dangerous parts of our journey. Keep your eyes peeled for the slave catchers."

Claire pulls her phone from her back pocket. "Still no reception."

Joy asks Claire, "What is that thing?"

"It's a phone."

"What do you do with it?"

"I talk to my best friend, Nell, and all the cute guys."

Rob chimes in, "Nell's eyebrows are so bushy she needs hedge shears to thin them out."

Jupiter and Caleb laugh.

Lucy howls.

Anna chastises, "Benji, keep that dog quiet."

Lucy barks again.

"What is it, girl?" Benji hopes to figure out what Lucy is trying to convey. "What's out there in the dark?"

"Slave catchers on horses with their dogs," Anna says.

Lucy growls again, and this time, without warning, she runs into the darkness and disappears into the forest.

Benji calls out, "Come back, Lucy, come back!"

Caleb tries to calm him. "She'll be back. She's a good dog, a brave dog."

Lucy has picked up the scent of the slave catchers and their dogs and is causing a diversion for the eight travelers to get through. Lucy attacks the lead dog and a fight ensues. She is soon outnumbered by the other dogs. She fights courageously before the number of dogs bests her, leaving her wounded. The slave catchers and their dogs eventually move on, leaving Lucy for dead. The travelers didn't realize that Beau Jamison had put a warrant out for Anna, Joy, Jupiter, Caleb, and Jennie. Beau is willing to pay two thousand dollars for the capture and return of all five of Gloria's children. Beau remembered how Anna had outsmarted him, and this time he hired the best slave catchers from out of state.

The group pushes onward to the next marker.

Benji is sobbing, "Where is Lucy? Doesn't anybody care?"

Jennie places her arm around Benji shoulders as they walk together.

Claire falls back with Jennie and Benji and tells him, "We will find Lucy, I promise."

Caleb stops short. "Do you hear that? It sounds like a whining animal. Over there! Right over there."

Caleb, Rob, and Benji run toward the whimpering sound. It is Lucy, blood-soaked and shaking. She can barely stand. Benji takes off his outer shirt and covers his dog.

Benji scolds her, "Why did you run off?"

Jupiter tries to comfort Benji. "You have a brave dog. She must have heard the Railroad men and their dogs and went out to distract them from us."

Anna kneels beside Jupiter and Benji. "Give the dog to Caleb. He can do miracles with animals."

Caleb bends down to examine Lucy. With water from his canteen, Caleb washes her wounds. Pulling a handful of berries from a bush, Caleb crushes the red berries and pats them into Lucy's wounds. He tears several strips of cloth from his shirt to bandage them.

Caleb steps back. "She's pretty beat up, but I think she'll be fine in a couple of days. We'll have to carry her or make a stretcher to transport her until she gets better."

Benji volunteers, "I'll carry her. She's my dog!"

Jennie prompts him gently, "I know you want to, but let Caleb and Jupiter make a stretcher. And if you want to, you and I can tote the stretcher together."

Benji smiles, "I'd like that very much."

Caleb and Jupiter cut down two nice trees for poles. Then they skin the tree barks to make straps. After fastening the straps to the poles, Caleb pulls a jacket out of his satchel for a cushion. Rob and Jupiter gently place Lucy on the stretcher. With Benji on one side and Jennie on the other, they carry Lucy to safety.

Anna tells Rob and Claire, "If anyone can nurse that dog back to health, it's Caleb."

Benji, Rob, and Claire thank Caleb and Jupiter for their care of Lucy.

"That boy sure loves that dog," remarks Joy.

Claire nods, affirming. "Ever since Mom and Dad brought Lucy home from the kennel, the two have been inseparable."

Bonds and friendships are beginning to emerge within the group: The youngest, Benji and Jennie; the fellas, Rob, Jupiter, and Caleb; the young women, Joy and Claire. The girls never stop talking. Anna occasionally joins the conversation, but she is mostly focused on the mission. Anna believes that the group is most vulnerable when they let their guard down. She is constantly reminding the group not to be distracted. Bad things could quickly happen when they are not paying attention.

Jupiter and Caleb are totally mesmerized by the 21st century technology Rob shares with them. Rob tells them that gas powered automobiles will replace the horse and wagon. He informs them about airplanes that will transport people from one city to another. Rob calls them flying birds carrying people. He explains to them that battles like the one they just saw will ultimately free the slaves. Jupiter and Caleb listen attentively while Rob talks, the eighteenth century fellas trying their best to make sense of every word he is saying.

Benji and Jennie carry the stretcher with Lucy on board. Caring for Lucy draws the two youngest travelers closer.

Chapter 6
We All Have Dreams

*J*ennie asks Benji, "What do you want to be when you grow up?"

"I don't know. I'm not very good at anything. Maybe a game developer."

"What's that?"

"Someone who makes up games for people to play."

"You make games for people and get paid for it?" Jennie is incredulous.

"Yes, you can. And you can make a lot of money."

"I'm convinced that whatever you do, you're going to be good at it. I watched how you care for Lucy. Your heart is in the right place, so I know you will be just fine."

Benji is touched. "Thanks, Jennie. You're a good friend."

"Don't get all soft on me, future boy."

Benji asks her in return, "What would you like to do when you grow up, Jennie?"

"I think I want to be a doctor. I see how my brother Caleb fixes animals, except I want to fix people."

Claire and Joy are immersed in deep conversation about slavery on the plantation. Joy tells Claire that slaves think about a lot of things besides work. "We think about love and courting, especially when a new boy comes to the plantation. On Sundays after church we sing and dance and cut the fool. On Christmas and Thanksgiving Day, Master Beau gives us extra food rations. I love baking. I bet I could make a mean apple pie from the fruit orchard we just left.

"Slaves instinctively know that abuse is wrong. We are just powerless to do anything about it." Joy continues, "Slaves are constantly told they are inferior people. Property, like a wagon or a dog. You tell someone that long enough, soon they start believing it. Momma never let us believe that lie. She would tell us that we are somebody. The women are expected to have children, work the fields, or serve in the main house. I learned to read and write from my momma, Gloria. She had to sneak and hide to teach us. Master Beau didn't want any of his slaves to be smarter than him. Many of the slaves heard about freedom but were not sure what it really meant."

"That is so sad."

"You don't know what you don't know." Changing the subject, Joy asks, "So, Claire, what do you want to be when you grow up?"

"I want to help people, like a mental health counselor of some kind."

Joy asks, "What is a mental health counselor?"

"Somebody who listens to other people's problems and helps them solve them."

"Girl, you gonna have a job forever, 'cause everybody's got problems."

Claire smiles. "So, Joy, what do you want to do first when you are free?"

"Oh, I'm not sure. First I want to breathe in the air of liberty, I want to see for myself how does free air feel. Secondly, it will be wonderful to have choices. Maybe I'll find me a nice, young, educated man, get married, and have some children," she laughs.

"Everybody down!" exclaims the always attentive Anna.

The sound of thundering hoofs is getting close. Horsemen that ride that aggressively at night have to be the slave catchers. The riders soon pass the eight travelers as they disappear into the night. The horses kick up so much dirt it leaves Benji and Jennie coughing.

"Get up," Anna says. "We must keep moving forward to the next marker before sunrise."

As the eight begin their walk, everybody is quiet. Caleb checks on Lucy periodically, occasionally changing her bandages. Lucy is getting stronger and more alert. Carrying Lucy around on a stretcher is kind of fun for Benji and Jennie, but with her return to heath, Lucy wants to walk on her own.

"Is that a light coming from over that hill?" asks Jupiter.

Rob says, "I think it is. But what would a light be doing in the midst of nowhere?"

Anna laughingly replies, "I said the exact same thing. It is the church in the middle of nowhere."

The group picks up their pace as they move closer to the church. Anna knocks on the door as the other seven observe. Anna knocks again, this time louder and harder. Still, no response at the door. After coming so far, disappointment fills the hearts of the travelers. What to do now? What could have happened to Walter and Janie Smalls? Why are they not answering the door? The tired, hungry, and thirsty travelers are left standing in the night, pondering their next move.

Anna says, "We can't stay out here in the open. Besides, it will be sunrise soon."

Jupiter sarcastically responds, "We know, Anna. We travel at night, and we rest during the day."

Anna ignores Jupiter's comment. Trying to put a positive look on their bleak situation, she mulls, "We are just twenty miles from freedom."

Just as the eight travelers are about to walk away, Claire speaks up. "Wait, everybody! I see a light. Someone is coming to the front door."

Jupiter, not believing Claire, hurries back to her point of view.

He excitingly confirms to Anna, "Somebody is coming, for real. Somebody with a light. Glory hallelujah, somebody is coming."

Just as Anna runs back to Claire and Jupiter, the door barely opens. A voice from inside speaks.

"Who is it, and what do you want?"

Anna whispers, "Minister Smalls, is that you?"

Not recognizing Anna's voice, Reverend Smalls retorts, "Who wants to know?"

"It's me, Anna Jamison. I ran away from my master over a year ago. You and Ms. Janie helped me and nine other runaways escape to freedom."

"I remember you, Anna. You came in here soaking wet, trembling like a little lamb. Come on in here, girl. And who are these with you?" The reverend yells, "Janie, put on lots of coffee!"

Ms. Janie appears. "Walter, what in the world is all this noise? Who are all these people?"

"You remember Anna?"

"I sure do. Let me look at you. You were a little bitty thing, soaking wet. Who are these others with you?"

Anna answers, "This is my big brother, Jupiter."

Jupiter nods, "Please to meet you, Ma'am."

Anna continues, "My sisters, Joy and Jennie."

They both in harmony say, "Pleased to meet you, Ma'am."

"My little brother, the animal fixer, Caleb."

Caleb responds respectfully, "Howdy."

"These are my newest friends, Claire, Rob, and Benji."

Claire, Rob, and Benji respond, "Hi…," slightly waving their hands.

Anna resumes gladly, "We cannot forget our wonder dog, Lucy."

"Well, hello," Reverend Smalls says to Lucy.

Lucy barks, now fully recovered and vigorously wagging her tail.

Ms. Janie says, "Everybody, come in and settle yourselves."

Ms. Janie begins to fix her signature breakfast: flapjacks, scrambled eggs, bacon, and potatoes. To drink, she makes four pitchers of sweet water and lemon.

Rob, stuffing his mouth says, "I wish my mom cooked like this." Benji nods his head in agreement.

Reverend Smalls speaks with annoyance. "The Railroad men have been at my door constantly. They have threatened me and Ms. Janie within an inch of our lives. Those hateful men set fire to our church, although it didn't do much damage. We trust that we are doing God's will. I believe God told me to build this church right here, twenty miles from freedom. Maybe one day, me and Ms. Janie will get to walk across that bridge to the promised land and stay. Until then, this our assignment."

After the travelers eat and refresh themselves, Reverend Smalls takes them to the basement to hide out until nightfall. Just as Anna and the group start to relax from the stress of being on the run, and now with full stomachs, nightfall comes.

Reverend Smalls says to the group, "I think it's safe to go now. Let's have prayer.

"Lord, protect these children from the evil men that would seek to harm them. Give them safe passage to freedom and for the rest of their lives. Bless them and help them to be a blessing."

Everyone says, "Amen!"

The eight travelers begin their last twenty miles from slavery to freedom. Without warning, everyone notices a distinct temperature drop. It is so noticeable that everybody can see the frost from their breath. This is no time to stop, even though Claire, Benji, and Jennie complain about their hands getting cold.

Chapter 7

Beau Jamison's Last Stand

"**E**verybody, get down!" Anna shouts. The sound of thundering hoofs of the Railroad men is so close that Anna and the group can view the men on the horses. One of the horsemen causes Anna to take a deep breath. She has always been the rock, the voice of reason and calm among the eight. These Railroad men are different, and Anna is visibly shaken. Anna always believed she could outmaneuver the Railroad men, but this time it feels different.

Joy worriedly asks, "What's wrong, Anna? What did you see?" Hesitating while regaining her composure, Anna says, "I think one of the men riding a horse is Beau Jamison."

Jupiter responds, "Say what?" Anna repeats herself. "Yes, I think one of the horsemen riding with the slave catchers is Beau Jamison."

Rob tries to remain calm, "Everybody takes a deep breath. It's gonna be alright. Anna, you brought us this far, and we trust you. Whatever happens is meant to happen, but we need you to lead us to freedom."

Jupiter agrees. "Rob is right," he reassures Anna. You're the only one who knows the way. We are with you, big sis, so, let's keep moving." Jupiter gives her a big smile and then pats Anna across her shoulder.

The eight travelers continue their walk, and then it begins to rain. The once dirt road gives away to a muddy marsh. The trees are swaying back and forth from the lively wind. It is hard to tell how far or how close the dogs are, but they can be heard in the distance.

Anna excitedly proclaims, "I can see the bridge from here. We are almost there. We've got to keep pushing." Then, she hears someone not from their group say, "Stop, don't make another move."

One of the men who sits upon a white horse looks right at them. Soon the hounding dogs catch up and force the eight against the edge of the river. The river bank is beginning to overflow. Anna looks over to the bridge and sees Beau Jamison. He sits on his prized mare as they stand on the wooden bridge.

The falling rain soaks his outer garment. Beau says to Anna, "You thought you could outsmart me, didn't you? Nobody outsmarts Beau Jamison. Now, you come home, and all will be forgiven. Your momma misses you. Hell, I miss you. Now, you and your kinfolk, come here!"

Anna defiantly replies, "Master Beau, we're not coming with you, now or ever."

Beau thunders, "What you mean Anna? I own you!"

Anna sharply responds to Beau, "You don't own me no more. I got papers making me free and my kinfolk are coming with me across that bridge you standing on. You're the only one standing between us and freedom."

"You know I could kill all of you and nobody would say a word. Shoot, nobody would even miss you, except maybe your momma." He laughs to himself.

Anna stands her ground. "You and those horrible Railroad men might overpower us, but I swear I will kill you dead, Beau Jamison." Anna promptly pulls a pistol from her satchel. "Now are you going to let us by? Or will I have to put a lead ball in your chest?"

Before Anna can finish her sentence, ear-piercing thunder cracks across the sky followed by several intense flashes of lightening. The winds and rain pick up fiercely. This time, the rain is accompanied by sleet and hail. The hailstones are so large they looked the size of silver dollars falling from the sky. The hailstones spook Beau's horse, making her uncontrollable. Beau's unstable mare rears up, throwing him from the saddle. Just as Beau gets to his feet, the frightened horse rears again, hitting him in the chest and knocking him over the rails of the bridge into the river. The Railroad men try to rescue Beau, but the rushing force of the river is too strong. The last Anna and her fellow travelers see of Beau, he is heading downstream.

The eight travelers make it to the bridge and cross over to freedom. All eight climb to the top of this huge hill. When at the top, they run to the side door of this enormous white house. They all knock on the door. As they continue knocking, a light is seen coming toward them. A voice calls out from behind the door asking, "Who is it?"

Anna replies, "It's me, Mr. Willingham, and I have brought my kinfolks and some friends with me."

Mr. Willingham says, "Come on in, Anna! Bertie and I have been waiting for your return."

Chapter 8

Home
At
Last

*A*s soon as Anna her fellow travelers step through the door, the light from Mr. Willingham's lantern becomes intensely brighter until it is impossible to see anyone in the room. Along with the intense light comes a boisterous wind that surrounds Claire, Rob, Benji, and Lucy.

Claire fearfully speaks, "What is happening?"

Rob replies, "I don't know, but it feels eerily familiar. My hands and my face feel weird."

"It's de ja vu," chimes in Benji.

Lucy barks.

All of a sudden, the three James kids find themselves back in the cellar of the library.

Rob speaks, "Where did everybody go? Where's Anna, Jupiter, Joy, Caleb, and Jennie?"

"I don't know, maybe it was what Benji said. Maybe we were time travelers and this basement was some kind of portal to another time." Claire looks around and continues, "Enough of this weird time traveling stuff. July 4, 2020 is going to look so amazing."

All three James kids rapidly climbed the stairs, all knocking on the door and yelling, "Mr. Washington! Mr. Washington? Mr. Washington!" Mr. Washington answers the door and all three kids rush out, almost knocking him down.

Claire declares, "We are home!" She is laughing, screeching, and hugging her siblings. Even Mr. Washington, with that twinkle in his eyes, smiles.

Lucy barks, swiftly wagging her tail.

"Wow! Can you believe it? That was so cool!" Benji yells.

Rob joins with excitement, "Now, that was so dope!" He laughs. "So very dope."

Ms. Peters shushes them. "Children, remember, this is a library. Keep your voices down. Did you enjoy your adventure?"

"Yes!" all three say, ignoring the quiet protocol.

Rob adds, "That was so crazy." He turns around, shaking his head and hands in disbelief.

Ms. Peters graciously informs them, "The library is not just a place for old books. It's a place where imaginations and adventures begin."

Mom walks in, apologizing to Ms. Peters. "I hope they were not too much trouble."

Ms. Peters responds with a smile and a twinkle in her eye, "They were just fine."

"Mom, Mom! You won't believe where we went!" Benji excitedly exclaims as they walk out of the library.

Rob looks back as he walks away. "Hey, Mr. Washington! We'll be back."

About The Author

*J*ohn is a Christian, a husband, a father, and a retired 26-year United States Air Force Veteran. John's wide professional background includes the following: Youth pastor, Industrial Engineer, Meteorologist, and Industrial Arts Teacher.

John's love for travel, science fiction, and United States history is evident in his writings.